We hope you enjoy this book.
Please return or renew it by the due date.
You can renew it at www.norfolk.gov.uk/libraries
or by using our free lib...
phone 0344 800 8...
card and pin re...
...an si...

My Grandma and Me

MINA JAVAHERBIN

illustrated by
LINDSEY YANKEY

WALKER BOOKS
AND SUBSIDIARIES
LONDON • BOSTON • SYDNEY • AUCKLAND

WHEN I WAS GROWING UP IN IRAN,
my grandma lived with us. I followed
her everywhere. When she swept,
I swept. When she cooked, I cooked.
When she prayed, I prayed like
her, too.

At dawn, when she woke up for namaz, I woke up with her, too.
"Praying at dawn is my favourite," she would say with a smile.
"Mine, too!" I would say with a wider smile.

Because only the two of us were up at that time, and no one was there to stop me, I would climb up and lie on her back while she prayed.

My grandma never told me to stop or broke out of her prayers. Instead, she sat up gently each time, making sure that I didn't fall.

After her namaz, we kept watch for the bread delivery boy. He piled the bread high on his bike like a clever acrobatic act.

But my grandma and I had a clever act, too. We bought fresh bread every day without leaving our third-floor apartment!

We sent our baskets down with ropes, the bread boy placed the bread inside, and then we hauled them up.

My grandma's basket was so big, I could fit inside it. I would sit in that basket and pretend to be flying my own plane.

My doll played, too.

Once the bread arrived, my doll, my grandma and I
would take some to my friend Annette, next door.

Like Annette and me, our grandmas were best friends. They enjoyed each other's company. Every day while we played together, they talked, laughed and drank coffee.

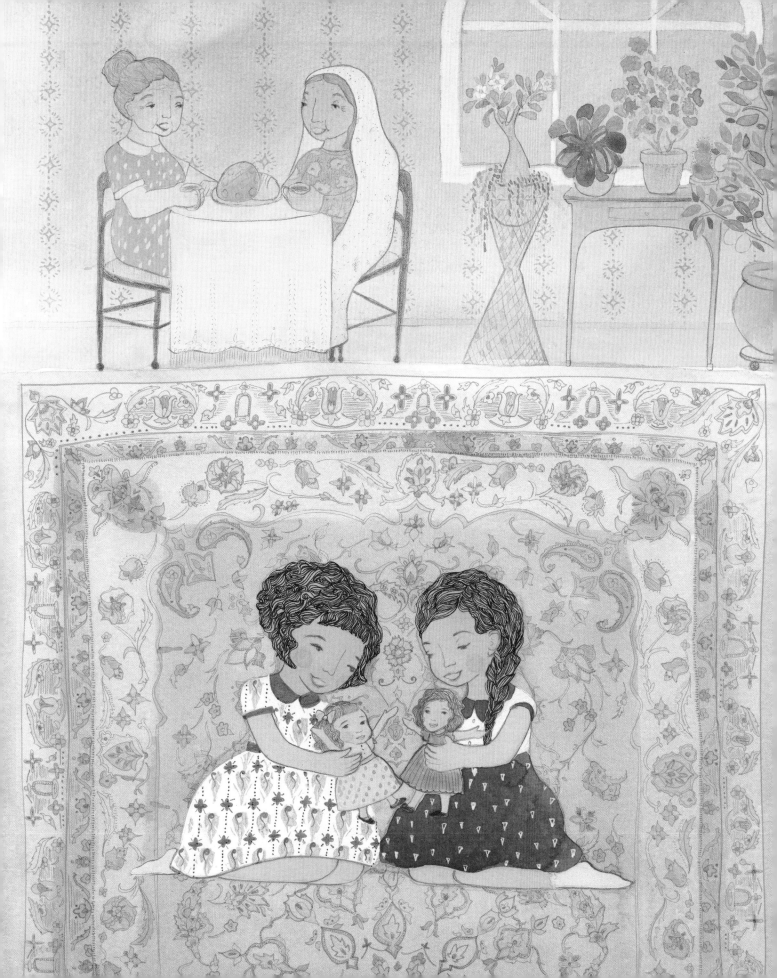

Our grandmas knitted blankets together
as they watched us play hopscotch in the alley.
They donated them to my grandma's mosque
and Annette's grandma's church.

From the end of the alley, we could see their heads
bent over the blankets – Annette's grandma with her
silver hair and my grandma in her favourite chador,
the white one with small purple flowers.

My grandma had all kinds of chadors. She wore them for different occasions. For parties and mosque, she wore a black one, made of fancy crepe fabric. It was heavy, soft and cool to the touch. It looked like a magical cape. My grandma sewed all her own chadors.

And I helped.

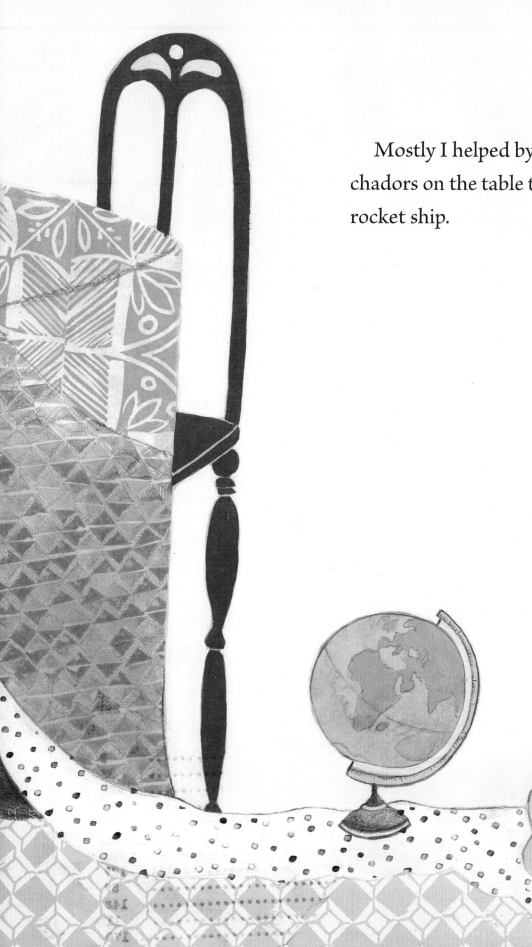

Mostly I helped by draping her chadors on the table to build my rocket ship.

Or tying her chador around my neck so I could fly from the moon to planets. I was a super-astro-explorer! My grandma was always waiting for me back at the base camp with cookies. We ate together while I told her about my space adventures.

During the holy month of Ramadan, my grandma did not eat from dawn to dusk. When she woke up to eat, before sunrise, I woke up to eat, too.

"You're too young to fast just yet," she said to me. I ate with my grandma anyway. Then I ate as usual during the day. And after dusk, at iftar time, I ate with her again!

One time, when I was a little older and finally fasted with her, in the middle of the dark and sombre night, I wore the chador she made me and we walked together to the mosque.

Inside, the lights shone bright, and no one was quiet or sombre. People laughed and ate and talked until it was time for prayers. My grandma prayed for Annette's grandma. She prayed that Annette's grandma would go to heaven.

After the prayers, there was
tea and milk and dates and sherbet
and cookies. In the mosque's
kitchen, volunteers cooked rice and
stew in giant copper pots. Some ate
at the mosque, while others took
the food home. We filled a dish,
and on the way home, my grandma
left it for a man sleeping on the
pavement. As we walked away, she
said a prayer for the sick and poor
in the world.

The next morning when I saw Annette, she whispered a secret to me: "Last night at the church, my grandma prayed for your grandma to go to heaven!"

My eyes widened. "My grandma did the same thing at the mosque!"

Annette and I looked up. Our grandmas were talking and drinking coffee together. I could imagine them knitting and laughing together anywhere – on Earth, on Mars, or in heaven.

In this big universe full of many
moons, I have travelled and seen
many wonders, but I've never
loved anything or anyone the way
I loved my grandma. She was
kind, generous and full of love.
I still want to be just like her.

To my beloved grandma Batool
M. J.

To Ashton
L. Y.

AUTHOR'S NOTE

As in most cultures, Iranians use various terms or endearing names for their grandmothers. The most usual one is *maman-bozorg*, which just means "grandma". My grandpa used to call my grandma *Khanom*, which means "lady", to show his respect for her, and so my father and uncle grew up calling her that as well. And when I came along, I called her *Khanom*, too. To me, my grandma was indeed a lady – noble, dignified, graceful and kind.

ILLUSTRATOR'S NOTE

I have been blessed with two grandmas in this life, and illustrating Mina's story has stirred up my own fond memories. I will always remember my grandma Brooks's hoot of laughter and her kindness. And with each visit, I admire the twinkle in my grandma Jeanne's eyes when my son blows her a kiss.

First published 2019 by Walker Books Ltd
87 Vauxhall Walk, London SE11 5HJ

This edition published 2020

10 9 8 7 6 5 4 3 2 1

Text © 2019 Mina Javaherbin
Illustrations © 2019 Lindsey Yankey

The right of Mina Javaherbin and Lindsey Yankey to be identified as the author and illustrator respectively of this work has been asserted by them in accordance with the Copyright, Designs and Patents Act 1988

This book has been typeset in Brioso Medium

Printed in China

All rights reserved. No part of this book may be reproduced, transmitted or stored in an information retrieval system in any form or by any means, graphic, electronic or mechanical, including photocopying, taping and recording, without prior written permission from the publisher.

British Library Cataloguing in Publication Data: a catalogue record for this book is available from the British Library

ISBN 978-1-4063-9083-4

www.walker.co.uk